Help
Vikir

Written by Adam and Charlotte Guillain

Chapter 1: A Viking Longship

"Maybe we can find something in the shop later for our holiday challenge," said Asha, as she, Finn, Tess and Rav walked into the museum. Their teacher had set the class a challenge to collect six objects over the summer.

While Tess and Asha went to try on Viking costumes, Finn and Rav went to look at a longship.

"It's a replica of a ship in a museum in Norway," read Rav.

"What an amazing carving!" said Finn, running his fingers over the dragon's head carved into the wood.

As he touched the longship, the lights in the room began to flash. Then it went dark, and the boys felt themselves whirling away.

Light hit the boys' faces and they looked around, feeling dazed.

"Where are we this time?" murmured Rav.

They were standing on a grassy slope by a river. Down by the water, they could see a group of men, busy hammering wood.

"It looks like the longship in the museum," said Rav. "Hang on – you don't think they're Vikings, do you?"

Finn gulped. He'd read that Vikings were fearsome warriors.

"Maybe we should hide," he whispered.

"Too late," said Rav. A boy was running up the hill towards them.

Chapter 2: Back to the Vikings

"Are you here to help?" panted the boy. "We're desperate."

"We can try," said Finn, glancing down at the men hammering below them.

"You must," said the boy. "We're going to be in big trouble if we don't finish the ship in time."

Finn and Rav introduced themselves to the boy, who said his name was Eric.

As Eric led them down the hill he whispered, "The village chief is angry because we're late. The ship must be ready to sail to find new land before winter comes."

Eric took them to his father. "More help. Just what we need," he said, as he handed each of the boys a hammer and a bag of wooden pegs.

Eric showed Rav and Finn where to knock the wooden pegs into place. They began to join in and slowly the ship started to look more like the one in the museum. Everyone around them was working silently, with the sound of hammering echoing around the valley.

It was hard work. Rav paused to get his breath back and Eric looked up.

"Don't stop!" he whispered urgently. "We don't have time for a rest!"

Then the air was shattered as a loud booming voice shouted, "Haven't you finished yet?"

Chapter 3: Chief Olaf

Finn and Rav peered over the side of the ship. A huge man with a yellow beard was striding over to the longship with a look of thunder on his face.

"We must sail this evening," he bellowed. "Or you will all be punished!"

Eric's father stood up straight. "We will be ready, Chief Olaf," he called in a calm voice. None of the other Vikings were looking at the chief.

Olaf frowned and stomped to the front of the ship. "You haven't carved the figurehead yet," he shouted. "It needs to be fearsome enough to terrify my enemies."

Eric's father put his hand on the shoulder of a pale, trembling Viking. "Halvar is ready to carve the figurehead," he said. "It's going to be hideously scary."

Chief Olaf grunted and turned to march back to the village. The Viking called Halvar let out a shaky breath.

The Vikings went back to work on the ship immediately. Eric's father glanced over at Rav and Finn and called to Eric, "Your friends look tired and hungry. Take them home to eat and come back quickly."

Eric led Finn and Rav away from the river towards a cluster of buildings.

Chapter 4: Help for Halvar

Eric took Rav and Finn through the village. "This is my house," he said, leading them inside a small building. There was one room, full of smoke from the fire.

"Mother, these are my friends who've been helping us build the ship," said Eric to a woman with a giant piece of cloth.

"You must eat quickly," said Eric's mum.

She went to the fire and stirred a pot sitting above the flames. Then she scooped stew into four bowls and passed them round. Eric broke a loaf of bread and handed Rav and Finn chunks to eat.

"It's tasty!" said Finn, raising his eyebrows.

Thanks!

They gobbled down the stew and then Eric's mum gathered up the cloth she had been weaving.

"This is the sail for the new ship," she told Rav and Finn. "It's ready now."

They rolled up the sail and the three boys carried it out of the house and back through the village together.

As they hurried down towards the river, they could see the men had fixed the mast on the longship.

"The sail!" cried Eric's dad. They unfurled the woven cloth and the men attached ropes to fix it to the mast.

Halvar was staring at the front of the ship and frowning.

Rav and Finn walked over to Halvar. "What are you going to carve?" asked Rav.

Halvar sighed. "I don't know. I've run out of ideas. And I'm terrified it won't be fierce enough for Chief Olaf."

He ran his hand through his hair and the boys could see he was shaking.

As the sail was raised, the sun burst through the clouds and lit up the red and white stripes on the cloth. Feeling hot, Finn wiped his brow and pulled his jumper off.

Halvar stared at Finn and raised his arms in the air.

Chapter 5: Finn's Dragon

Halvar pointed at Finn's T-shirt.

"This picture!" he shouted. "It's perfect!"

Finn looked down and remembered he was wearing his kung fu club T-shirt. It had a picture of a roaring dragon on it.

"Stand there!" Halvar ordered Finn, and he started to carve.

Finn stood still while Rav, Eric and the others rolled logs between the ship and the water's edge.

"What are they for?" Finn asked Halvar.

"Wait and see," answered Halvar with a grin, as he carved sharp fangs in the dragon's mouth. He blew away the wood shavings and beamed at Finn.

"The ship is ready!" shouted Halvar. The other Vikings ran across to look at his figurehead. They cheered heartily and congratulated Halvar and Finn.

Then silence fell. Finn and Rav turned to see Chief Olaf stomping towards them.

He glared up at the figurehead without speaking.

Chief Olaf threw his head back and roared. Finn gulped and grabbed Rav's arm as Olaf stomped towards Halvar.

"What's he going to do?" thought Finn.

"You have made me proud, Halvar!" boomed Olaf, clapping Halvar round the shoulders and beaming.

This is the fiercest figurehead I have ever seen!

"The ship is ready, Chief Olaf," said Eric's father proudly.

"Then we must launch it!" yelled Olaf.

The men stood on either side of the ship and began to push it forwards.

"So that's what the logs are for!" shouted Finn, as the ship began to roll down the slope towards the river.

With a mighty splash, the longship rolled into the water.

"Climb in," urged Eric, gesturing to Finn and Rav to follow the men who were leaping on board. The three boys clambered on to the ship and watched the villagers wave from the shore as the sail billowed in the wind.

"How do you steer the ship?" Rav asked Eric.

"There's a steering oar at the back," said Eric, leading Rav towards it.

Meanwhile, Finn stood in the sunshine and looked up at the figurehead. He was plunged into shadow as Chief Olaf appeared behind him.

"What is your name?" he demanded, glaring at Finn. Finn's knees buckled as he stammered the answer. Chief Olaf bellowed to the rest of the crew, "Our new longship has a name. We shall call it *Finn's Dragon*."

The other Vikings cheered and lifted Finn on to their shoulders.

As the ship surged towards the sea, the sky darkened. Rav turned to Eric and said, "I think it's time for us to go."

Eric looked confused as Finn and Rav started to whirl away. "Goodbye!" he called. "Thank you for your help!"

Finn and Rav opened their eyes in the bright light of the museum. Finn put his hands in his pockets and gasped. "A wooden peg from the ship!" he cried, holding it up to show Rav. "What a great memory for my summer challenge!"

Help the Vikings

What other things will the Comet Street Kids collect for their holiday challenge? Read the other books in this band to find out!

Help the Vikings

The Summer Fete

At the Seaside

The Laughing Kookaburra

The Sleepover

Asteroid Alarm!

Talk about the story

Answer the questions:

1 What was the name of the Viking boy that Finn and Rav met?

2 What did Rav and Finn do to help build the longship?

3 What does the word 'urgently', on page 9, mean?

4 Why was the village chief angry?

5 Why did Eric's mother want the children to eat their stew quickly?

6 Can you explain in your own words what happened in Chapter 5?

7 What would you have done if you were Rav and Finn? Would you have helped the Vikings?

8 Would you have liked to live in Viking times? Why? Or why not?

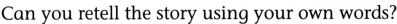

Can you retell the story using your own words?